Tom and Ricky

and the

Flying Wheel Mystery

Bob Wright

High Noon Books
Novato, California

Cover Design: Nancy Peach
Interior Illustrations: Herb Heidinger

Glossary: picture, camera, ticket, fence, film, uncle, tool

International Standard Book Number: 0-87879-361-5

9 8 7
5 4 3 2 1 0 9

Contents

CHAPTER 1

A New Camera

Tom went over to Ricky's house. He knew it was Ricky's birthday. He wanted to see his friend. He wanted to surprise Ricky.

Ricky opened the door. All of a sudden there was a bright light. Tom jumped back.

Ricky was standing in the door. He laughed. Then he said, "I'm sorry, Tom. I didn't mean to make you jump. I just wanted to surprise you. I took your picture."

He was holding a camera in his hands.

"You sure did surprise me. I didn't even know you had a camera," Tom said.

Ricky showed Tom the camera. "My mom gave it to me for my birthday. I have wanted a camera for a long time. My mom knew that, so she gave me one," Ricky said.

"And you were trying it out," Tom said.

"Yes. I was taking pictures of Patches. Then I saw you coming. I thought it would be fun to take your picture, too," Ricky answered.

Ricky's dog Patches came running out. He barked and wagged his tail when he saw Tom.

"Let me get a picture of you and Patches," Ricky said. He held the camera to his eye and took another picture.

Patches wanted to play with the camera. He jumped up at it. "Stop that, Patches. Get down! Now look what you have done," Ricky said.

"What did he do?" Tom asked.

"He marked up the camera," Ricky answered.

Tom looked. "It's not a bad mark. The camera is OK," he said.

"You're right. But I still wish he had not done that," Ricky said.

"Never mind. Happy birthday, Ricky. I came here to surprise you. But you surprised me first," Tom said.

"How were you going to surprise me?" Ricky asked his friend.

"I have a birthday present for you, too," Tom answered. He gave Ricky a ticket.

"What's this?" Ricky asked.

"It's a ticket to the big car race on Saturday. I have one, too. So we can go to the race together," Tom answered.

"Thanks a lot. But how did you get the money to buy these tickets?" Ricky asked.

"I didn't have to buy them. My Uncle Joe gave them to me. He is going to drive in the race," Tom answered.

"I didn't know you had an uncle who races cars," Ricky said.

"Yes. Uncle Joe lives in another town. He came here just for the race," Tom answered.

"Is he a good driver?" Ricky asked.

"He sure is. Uncle Joe is one of the best. He wins a lot of races. His picture is in the paper all the time," Tom answered.

"How come you never told me about your Uncle Joe before?" Ricky asked.

"You never asked me!" Tom answered.

Both boys laughed.

Then Ricky said, "It will be a lot of fun to see a car race. I have never seen one before."

"Be sure to take your new camera. You can get some good pictures on Saturday," Tom said.

CHAPTER 2

At the Race Track

The car race track was just outside of town. Tom and Ricky rode their bikes there on Saturday morning.

People had come from all over to see the big race. The two boys had to stand in line to get into the track.

Ricky and Tom gave their tickets to the man at the gate. The man said, "You have red tickets. You must know someone who is racing here today."

"What do the red tickets mean?" Ricky asked.

"They mean that you can go down to where the race cars are. You can watch the drivers get their cars ready for the race," the man answered.

"Everyone else has to watch from the seats around the track," Tom added.

"I can get some good pictures of the cars up close," Ricky said.

The man said, "Yes, you can. But be careful. And stay out of the way. They have a lot to do to get ready."

"Come on, Ricky. Let's go find Uncle Joe. He must be getting his car ready now," Tom said.

The boys went off to where the cars were.

The race cars were on one side of the track. There was a fence around them. Tom and Ricky looked through the fence. They could see men working on their race cars.

They walked over to a gate in the fence. A man in a white hat was standing there. The boys started to walk past him. He stopped them. "You cannot go in there. This part is only for drivers and friends of the drivers," he said.

Tom showed the man his red ticket. So did Ricky. Then Tom said, "My Uncle Joe is one of the drivers in the race."

The man looked at the red tickets. Then he said, "OK. You can go in."

"Now let's find my Uncle Joe," Tom said.

"OK. But let's look around first."

"All right," Tom answered.

"Look at all the racing cars! They're all over the place," Ricky said.

The cars were in all colors. Each one had a big number painted on the side. Ricky started to take pictures of all the cars.

Ricky took picture after picture. Soon, he was out of film. He took the old roll out of the camera. He put another roll of film in.

"I'm glad I bought two rolls of film. These pictures are going to be good," Ricky said.

Then Ricky walked over to a white racing car. It had a big number *1* painted on the side. "That car looks really fast," he said.

Tom looked at it, too. "It is. That's Al Hill's car. Al Hill is a good driver. A lot of people think that he will win the race today," he said.

"I thought you said your Uncle Joe was the best driver here," Ricky said.

"I said that he is very good. But Al Hill is just as good. And there are many other good drivers here today, too," Tom answered.

"This race should be a good one," Ricky said.

"Yes. And the driver who wins will get a lot of money," Tom answered.

CHAPTER 3

Before the Race

"Look! There's my Uncle Joe," Tom said to Ricky. Tom's uncle was working on his car. It was a blue car with number *26* painted on the side.

The boys walked over to Tom's uncle. Tom said, "Hello, Uncle Joe. This is my friend Ricky."

Uncle Joe turned to Ricky. "Glad to meet you," he said.

"Thanks for the free ticket." Ricky said.

"Are you ready for the race?" Tom asked his uncle.

"Just about. But we still have to put a new spring on the back of the car," Uncle Joe answered.

"We? Do you want us to help you do it?" Ricky asked.

"No. I have two helpers, Frank and Harry. They have gone to get the spring. They will help me when they get back," Uncle Joe said.

"How will you put the spring on?" Ricky asked.

Uncle Joe showed them a big box of tools behind the car. "We have all the tools that we need right there," Uncle Joe answered.

Then Uncle Joe started to get under his racing car. "I haven't got much time to talk right now. My helpers will be back with that spring soon. I'll start taking the old one off," he said.

"We'll stay out of your way. But let us know if we can help," Tom said.

"Is it all right if I take some pictures?" Ricky asked.

"Oh, sure. Go right ahead," Joe answered. He got under the car and started to work. He had a lot to do.

Ricky backed up to take a picture of Uncle Joe's car. He watched as a man walked over to Uncle Joe's tool box. "That must be one of Uncle Joe's helpers," he thought.

Just then Ricky took a picture. The camera made a bright light. The man by the tool box looked up. He looked surprised.

The man by the tool box looked up. He looked surprised.

Then another man walked over. He was carrying a big spring. "Here it is, Joe," the man said.

Uncle Joe came out from under the car. "Thanks, Frank. Let's start putting it on. Where's Harry?"

"He's getting something else," Frank said.

The men started to put the new spring on Uncle Joe's car. Tom and Ricky watched. Ricky took some more pictures.

At last, the work was done. Uncle Joe came out from under the car. "Now, we are all set. The car is ready to race," he said.

"Do you like to race cars? It must be fun," Ricky said.

"It is. But people who race cars can get hurt. Sometimes they can be killed," Joe answered.

Ricky looked inside the car. He wished that he was old enough to race a car like this.

Uncle Joe saw him looking at the car. "Would you like to sit behind the wheel, Ricky?" he said.

"Can I? Thanks!" He put his camera down and got into the racing car.

Uncle Joe and the others stood around. Joe told Ricky and Tom how the car worked. Then Tom said, "Let me take your picture behind the wheel, Ricky."

"Great! My camera is on the ground behind you," Ricky answered.

CHAPTER 4

The Film Is Spoiled

Tom looked for the camera. But it was not on the ground. "Your camera isn't here. Someone has taken it," he said to Ricky.

"My new camera! Quick! Let's try to find it." Ricky jumped out of the racing car.

Then Tom saw a man standing by a red racing car. The man was holding Ricky's camera. He was opening it up.

"Stop! That's my camera," Ricky yelled at the man.

17

"No, it's not. This is my camera," the man answered.

"Don't open the back. You will spoil the film," Ricky said.

But it was too late. The man had the back of the camera open. The light spoiled the film.

"What did you do that for?" Ricky said.

"I was going to put a new roll of film in. I told you, this is my camera," the man said.

Ricky showed him the mark on the camera. "Look at that. My dog made that mark. This has to be my camera," Ricky said.

The man looked at the mark. Then he gave the camera back. "Well, I thought it was mine. It looks the same," he said.

"You spoiled the film," Ricky said.

The man took out some money and gave it to Ricky. He said, "Buy another roll of film then. I thought that the camera was mine. I have one just like it."

Ricky was mad. But he took the money. Then Tom and Ricky walked back to talk to Uncle Joe. "Did he say he was sorry for spoiling your film?" Uncle Joe asked Ricky.

"No, he didn't," Ricky answered.

"I'm not surprised. I know that man. His name is Ken Martin. That red car, number 9, is his. No one likes him very much," Uncle Joe said.

"Why is that?" Tom asked.

Uncle Joe answered, "Ken Martin will do anything to win a race. He does not care about anyone but himself."

"Well, I hope that he loses today," Tom said to his uncle.

Then Ricky said, "I'll have to go to buy some more film. I'll be right back."

Ricky left. It wasn't long before he was back with a new roll of film. "Now let's get some more pictures before the race starts," he said.

Uncle Joe looked up at a big clock. It was on the wall of a tall house by the track. He said, "We don't have much time. The race is going to start soon. And I want to wash this dirt off my hands first. Watch my car. I'll be right back."

"Let me just get one picture of you and Tom," Ricky said to Uncle Joe.

Ricky took the picture.

"Let me just get one picture of you and Tom."

Then Uncle Joe went off to wash his hands. He wasn't gone long.

When Uncle Joe came back, it was time for the race to start. Frank and Harry helped him get into the car. Tom and Ricky watched. "Good luck, Uncle!" Tom said.

Uncle Joe waved and started his car. It started with a roar. The boys watched as Uncle Joe's car rolled onto the race track.

The other racing cars were also on the track now. The race was about to begin.

CHAPTER 5

The Flying Wheel

There were a lot of cars on the race track. They were in rows. All of them were ready to go.

Three cars were in the first row. First was Al Hill's white car, number *1*. Next to it was Ken Martin's red car, number *9*. Then came Uncle Joe's blue car, number *26*.

A man stood by the track. He was holding a green flag. Everyone was watching him. The man waved the green flag and the cars started off. The race was on!

Al Hill moved out in front. His car was very fast. Uncle Joe was right behind him. He was in second place. Then came Ken Martin's car.

Tom and Ricky watched as the cars went round and round the race track. "Come on, Uncle Joe!" Tom yelled.

Uncle Joe started to move up. So did Ken Martin in the red car. Then Ken and Uncle Joe were side by side.

All of a sudden, Ken Martin's car hit Uncle Joe's car. They were both going very fast. Joe's car went right off the track.

"He pushed him off the track!" Ricky yelled.

"What's going on?" Tom yelled.

But Uncle Joe got right back in the race. Soon he was right behind Ken Martin again.

The race went on. Al Hill was still in front. Now Ken Martin was in second place. Uncle Joe was close behind. And he was getting closer.

But the race was almost over. Uncle Joe would have to go very fast to pass Ken. Then he would have to pass Al Hill to win.

Just then, Al Hill's car started to move from side to side. "What's going on?" Ricky asked.

"Look at Al Hill! One of his wheels is coming off!" Tom answered.

The right front wheel of Al's car came flying off. Al Hill could not drive the car. It was going all over the track. He hit the track wall.

Some men went running over to Al Hill's car. They pulled Al out.

But the race went on. Now Ken Martin was in front. Uncle Joe was right behind.

Around and around they went. Uncle Joe tried to pass Ken. But Ken would not let him go by.

Then the race was over. Ken Martin had won. Uncle Joe was second.

Ken got out of his racing car. He went over to Mr. Ross, the track owner. He wanted to get the money for winning the race.

But Mr. Ross said, "We cannot give you the money just yet. We have to find out about Al's car."

"What do you mean? Give me the money! I won the race!" Ken said.

"What's this all about?" Ricky asked.

"And there is a name on the tool. It is Joe's tool."

Mr. Ross answered, "Someone made the wheel fly off of Al Hill's car. That person wanted to make sure Al would not win the race."

Ken said, "It wasn't me!"

"Then who was it?" Mr. Ross asked.

"I think I know. It was Joe. I saw him by Al Hill's car before the race. He did it!" Ken said.

Everyone went over to Al Hill's car. Ken looked inside. "Look. There is a tool inside. Someone used that tool to make Al's wheel fly off. And there is a name on the tool. It is Joe's tool!" he said.

CHAPTER 6

Did Uncle Joe Do It?

The tool had Joe's name on it. Everyone stopped. They all looked at him.

"I didn't do it. I wouldn't do anything like that," Joe said.

"But this is your tool," Mr. Ross answered.

"Yes, it is. Someone must have taken it. Someone wanted to make it look like I did it," Uncle Joe said.

Mr. Ross said, "I don't believe you, Joe. This is your tool. So you must have done it."

"I didn't!" Uncle Joe said.

"If you did, you will never race again," Mr. Ross said.

"How can you be sure that I did it?" Joe said to Mr. Ross.

Ken Martin answered. He said, "I saw you by Al Hill's car just before the race. I saw you with that tool in your hand."

"Let's ask Al Hill about that," Uncle Joe said.

They went over to see Al Hill. He was not hurt. But he was mad. "Someone did this to my wheel before the race. I could have been killed."

"When do you think someone could have done it?" Tom asked.

Al thought. Then he said, "It must have been around 11 or 11:15. No one was watching the car then."

"Why not?" Mr. Ross asked.

"My helpers and I left to look at the track. We always do that before a race," Al answered.

Mr. Ross turned to Uncle Joe. He asked, "Where were you between 11 and 11:15?"

Joe said, "I was getting ready for the race. I was by my car. There wasn't much time. I went off to wash my hands."

Ricky said, "That's right. We saw Joe go off to wash his hands."

Mr. Ross asked, "What time was that?"

"I'm not sure," Ricky answered.

Ken said, "Well, I am sure. I saw Joe by Al's car at 11:10. I looked at my watch. So I know. Al's car was right next to mine."

Mr. Ross said, "Joe, I am surprised. I never thought that you would do something like this. I will make sure that you never race again."

"Mr. Ross gave Ken Martin the money for winning the race. Then everyone went home.

On the way home Ricky said, "Maybe your uncle did do it. He was gone just before the race. He told us he was going to wash his hands.

"I know my uncle wouldn't do anything like that," Tom said.

"Wait! I think that I have the answer," Ricky said.

"What do you mean?" Tom asked.

Ricky said, "I saw someone taking a tool from Uncle Joe's tool box. It was just before the race. I think that it was Ken Martin. I even took a picture of him taking the tool."

"But you don't have the picture. Don't forget, Ken opened your camera. He spoiled that roll of film," Tom answered.

Ricky said, "You're right. Now what do we do?"

CHAPTER 7

The Clock on the Wall

A few days later, Ricky went to visit Tom. "Do you have any news about your Uncle Joe?" he asked his friend.

Tom answered, "He is still trying to clear his name. He did not do anything to Al Hill's racing car. But no one believes him."

"You mean that they believe Ken Martin's story?" Ricky asked.

"Yes. And it was my uncle's tool they found in Al Hill's car," Tom answered.

"I'm sure that Ken put that tool in Al's car," Ricky said.

"So am I. But how can we make Mr. Ross believe us?" Tom said.

"I wish I knew," Ricky answered.

"My uncle has to clear his name. He will never race again. We have to help him," Tom said.

"Where is your uncle now?" Ricky asked.

"He is still at the track. There is going to be another race on Saturday. He wants to be in it. But first he has to clear his name," Tom answered.

"Let's go see him. Maybe we can help him show that Ken did it," Ricky said.

The boys got on their bikes. They went right to the track. They found Uncle Joe working on his racing car.

"Are you going to be in the next race after all?" Tom asked his uncle.

Uncle Joe answered, "I hope so. That is why I am getting the car ready. But Mr. Ross will not let me race until I clear my name."

Ricky said, "Would you like to see the pictures that I took last Saturday?"

They all looked at the pictures. One of the pictures showed Tom and his uncle by the racing car. Tom smiled. He said to Ricky, "You took this one just before the race started."

"Right," said Uncle Joe.

Ricky looked at the picture again. Then he said, "Look! The tall house in the back of the picture! There is a clock on the wall!"

"Look at the time on the clock. The clock shows 11:10."

"So what?" Tom asked.

"Look at the time on the clock. The clock shows 11:10," Ricky answered.

Tom smiled. He said to his uncle, "That was when Ken said he saw you by Al Hill's car. This picture shows that you were not by Al's car."

Uncle Joe said, "You're right!"

"If only I had that other picture. It would show who really broke Al's car," Ricky added.

"What do you mean?" Uncle Joe asked.

Ricky told Joe about the other picture. He told how he had taken a picture of Ken Martin. "Ken took your tool when you were under the car. He didn't think that anyone was watching your tool box. I have an idea," Ricky said.

CHAPTER 8

Ken is Caught

Ricky told more about his plan. He said, "We will need a room. I need some place to meet Ken Martin."

"There is a work room there. Will that do?" Uncle Joe asked.

"Let's take a look," Ricky said.

They looked at the work room. Then Ricky said, "This room will be fine. Now, here is what each of us will do. . ."

Ricky told the rest of his plan.

An hour later, they were ready. Tom went to look for Ken Martin. He found Ken by his red racing car.

Ken saw Tom coming. He said, "What do you want? Get out of here."

Tom said, "We know what you did. You took Uncle Joe's tool. You broke Al Hill's wheel. Ricky has a picture of you taking the tool. That will show that you did it."

Ken just laughed. He said, "You are trying to trick me. There is no picture. I made sure of that. I spoiled the film."

"That's what you think! The picture was on the first roll of film. You spoiled the second roll of film," Tom said.

Ken Martin just looked at Tom. He looked mad. Then he said, "It can't be. You are lying!"

Tom answered, "Am I? Ricky is here at the track. He has the picture. He is going to show it to Uncle Joe."

"Where is he?" Ken yelled.

"In the work room. My uncle will meet him there," Tom answered.

Ken pushed Tom to one side. He ran over to the work room.

Ricky was inside. "Give me that picture!" Ken yelled at him.

Ricky said, "What picture?"

"The picture that shows me taking Joe's tool," Ken answered.

"So you did do it!" Ricky said.

"Yes. But no one else will ever know. Not once I have that picture. Now give it to me!" Ken said. He picked up a metal bar. He was ready to hit Ricky with it.

Just then, Uncle Joe stepped out from behind a large box. "Put down that bar, Ken."

Al Hill and Mr. Ross also stepped out. Al said, "So it was you after all. I didn't think that Joe would do a thing like that. I could have been killed!"

"Your racing days are over," Mr. Ross said to Ken.

Ken said, "I was sure that I spoiled that film."

Tom said, "You did. But Ricky tricked you. He made you believe that he still had the picture."

"Put down that bar, Ken," he yelled.

Ricky asked Mr. Ross, "Who will get the money for winning the last race?"

"Joe will get it," Mr. Ross answered.

But Uncle Joe said, "No. Give it to Al. He would have won. But I will beat him in the next race."

Al Hill laughed. He said, "Maybe you will and maybe you won't. I'll see you on the track Saturday!"

"We will all be there!" Ricky said.

"Not Ken Martin!" Tom laughed.